Robinson's Hood

Jeff Gottesfeld

SADDLEBACK
PUBLISHING

ROBINSON'S HOOD

THE BANK OF BADNESS

CHOPPED

www.sdlback.com

Copyright ©2013 by Saddleback Educational Publishing

ISBN-13: 978-1-62250-000-0
ISBN-10: 1-62250-000-8
eBook: 978-1-61247-684-1

Printed in Guangzhou, China
NOR/1012/CA21201319

17 16 15 14 13   1 2 3 4 5

Chapter One

Robinson "Robin" Paige leaned his skinny self against the wall near the Barbara Jordan Community Center restrooms and rubbed his tired eyes. He was worn out, and not just from "Welcome Day" at Ironwood Central High School where he'd start ninth grade for real on Monday.

He was more than ready for school. He'd already done his summer reading, an amazing novel called *Bud, Not Buddy* about an orphan boy searching for family, and written a great five-paragraph essay too. Robin was whipped because he'd barely slept. There'd been a fist fight under his window at midnight that woke him the first time. An hour and a half later, there'd been another fight. This time it wasn't just gang dudes throwing punches.

This time, there'd been gunfire.

Three gunshots at one thirty in the morning can mess up your shut-eye, Robin thought.

Robin was no stranger to gunfire. He and his grandmother lived on the toughest street in the toughest hood in the tough city of Ironwood. Miz Paige—that's what everyone, except for Robin, called his grandmother—would have gotten them out of the Second Ward ages ago if she could afford it. She couldn't. She ran a joint on Ninth Street called the Shrimp Shack that was barely making it. Unless they hit the Powerball, they were stuck with the Ninth Street Rangers gang, the blast of

4

deuce-deuces at one thirty in the morning, the sirens. …

The men's room door opened. Old Mr. Smith teetered out. The Center had two kinds of members. You had to be younger than sixteen or older than sixty-five to hang out there. Robin was fourteen, though some folks still took him for twelve. Barely five feet tall, he had coal-colored skin and a buzz cut.

Mr. Smith was way older than sixty-five. He'd lost part of one foot in the Vietnam War, wore a special shoe on that foot, and sometimes used a cane. He had thick round glasses and smelled of Old Spice. Robin loved him. He used to be a locksmith and could open any lock with just a hairpin. He was great at games. He had taught Robin and his friends pinochle, hearts, spades, rummy. … Robin had never beaten Mr. Smith at cards. Not once. And checkers? Maybe twice.

"Robin Paige, you waitin' to walk me back to the rec room?"

Mr. Smith had on a baggy dress shirt tucked into pants, with his belt way too high. As for Robin, he wore the ICHS school uniform: dark blue pants and a matching short sleeve shirt. His new school had a strict dress code, mostly because so many kids got bussed there from different parts of the city. When the school first started, kids from the same hoods started dressing alike, and there were a lot of fights. That's when the school board said all Ironwood kids had to wear blue and blue, even the girls. Even the teachers.

Not that it stopped the fighting, Robin thought. *Kids know who's from their hood. You don't need a shirt to represent.*

"You got it, Mr. Smith." Then Robin noticed something. He winced. "Um … XYZ, Mr. Smith."

"XY. 'Scuse me, what?"

"XYZ, Mr. Smith. X-Y-Z."

Mr. Smith stared blankly. "Huh? Whatchu talkin' 'bout, Robin?"

Robin grinned and pointed. "X-Y-Z means examine your zipper."

Mr. Smith laughed. "Oh! Sorry. Don't want to be showin' the colors in the rec hall. Too many old ladies askin' me to marry them already." He zipped his fly. "Easy to fo'git when you my age."

Easy to forget, Robin corrected mentally. His gramma was always on his case about speaking properly, even if she used a lot of street slang herself. Robin could go both ways. It was useful.

"Okay," Mr. Smith said. "Sly's show starts in five minutes. It'll take me that long to git to the rec hall!"

Sly was Sylvester "Sly" Thomas. He was one of Robin's two homies, along with

Karen Knight, who everyone just called Kaykay. Sly's daddy was Reverend James "Tex" Thomas of the Ironwood Community Baptist Church that Robin and Miz Paige attended. Sly and Kaykay hung at the Center a lot. Most every Friday afternoon Sly put on a magic show. The old folks loved him. His goal was to have his own stage show in Las Vegas, and Robin thought he just might do it. He was a cold magician and a dope mime.

Robin and Mr. Smith finally reached the rec room, where a crowd of maybe fifty people waited near the low wooden stage for Sly to appear. Kaykay saw them enter. She rushed over with a full plate in her hands.

That's so Kaykay, Robin thought. *She never walks if she can run.*

Robin gulped. Kaykay was just so … fine, even in her blue school uniform. An inch taller than him, she had tawny skin, straight hair to her shoulders, and eyes that appeared to change color depending on her mood. Every boy who met her wanted to be with her. Robin did too.

Not that I'd ever tell her. She'd laugh her ass off.

"Robin! Mr. Smith! Check out what I made with Mrs. Swett in the kitchen!" Kaykay talked as fast as she moved. "Organic peanut butter cookies. Taste!"

That was so Kaykay too. She was all about keeping it organic and green. She was the kind of girl who'd yell at a stranger for dropping a McDonald's cup on the sidewalk.

Robin and Mr. Smith were about to try Kaykay's cookies when the room hushed. Robin thought Sly's show was starting, but it wasn't. Instead, a man of about forty-five took the stage. He wore black pants and a white shirt and stood ramrod straight. This was Sergeant Bruce Jones, who'd been a real Marine drill sergeant before he ran the Center. Everyone just called him Sarge. When Robin first met Sarge, he'd been afraid of him. Then he figured out that under it all, the ex-Marine was a softie.

"I'm gonna keep this short," Sarge declared, "'cause it sure ain't sweet. You know I care 'bout each of you. You also know the shape this place is in. We jus' got a visit from the city inspectors, and they say we can't put off the new roof no longer. But it's gonna cost twenty-five thousand dollars we ain't got. If we can't get the money soon, we gots to close."

A murmur went through the crowd. Robin felt sick to his stomach. The Center had to close? He loved this place. It had this rec hall, a kitchen, arts and crafts, meeting rooms, even a small library. The place was pretty jacked up, though. The heat was bad, the A/C worse. The walls and floors were a mess, and it did need a new roof in the worst way.

"When we gots to close?" Mr. Smith called out.

"Next Wednesday. Wednesday be the last day, 'less someone comes up with some big money. That's all I gotta say." Sarge stepped off the stage as everyone talked at once.

What will these old people do with themselves? Robin thought as a dozen conversations erupted around him. *What am I gonna do?*

Mr. Smith went to talk with some of his friends. Sly came over to join Robin and Kaykay. Sly wasn't tall, but he was wide. A clown by nature, he wasn't clowning now.

"Can you believe this bull?" Sly asked. "We can't let this place close! No way, no how!"

Kaykay put her hands on her hips. Robin thought that maybe she was about to cry. "Whatchu plannin' to do then, Sly? Pull a big-ass wad of dead presidents out your magic hat? If we was in the rich burbs, we'd get fixed right up. But who gonna help us out?"

"I wish I could," Sly admitted.

"We can't just give up," Robin told his friends. What they could do, he didn't know, but they just couldn't let the Center die.

Like Sly said: "No way, no how."

Chapter Two

Robin was still with Sly and Kaykay when he got a text from his grandma on his el-cheapo cell.

"heLP ME close shop?"

He managed a thin smile. His grandmother had fat fingers and never mastered the texting thing. He texted back.

"C U soon"

"I gotta help my grams," he told his friends. "Sly, why don't you do your magic show anyway? Cheer these folks up. And Kaykay? Pass out those cookies."

Robin headed out a moment later. The Center was on Marcus Garvey Boulevard

at Nineteenth Street, a fifteen minute walk
from his apartment above the Shrimp Shack.
Garvey wasn't just a main shopping street.
A lot of white folks used it as a way to get
home to the burbs when the highway got
jammed. Robin would see them hunched
over their steering wheels, safe behind the
locked doors of their Audis and Lexuses,
and wondered what they thought.

*Probably they're wondering how anyone
could live here. Probably they're thinking
how they're better than we are.*

Robin crossed Nineteenth. When he
reached the other side, he heard someone
shouting his name.

"Yo, Robin! Yo, Shrimp!"

He froze. "Shrimp" was the nickname
he'd been given in fourth grade by Tyrone
Davis because he was short and because his
grandmother ran the Shrimp Shack. Tyrone

had busted his chops constantly then and had been on his case ever since. These days, Tyrone was six feet tall, had a soul patch, and could kick Robin's ass from here to Chicago.

Robin kept it light as Tyrone approached. "Hey, wassup, Tyrone? How you doin'?"

Tyrone roared with laughter. He wore a black muscle shirt and sagging green shorts. "Ha! Shrimp talkin' like we be friends!"

"You all ready for school?" Robin asked, ignoring Tyrone's sarcasm.

"Only one thing good 'bout school and thas football, which you will never do, Shrimp. You be too shrimpy!"

Tyrone laughed again and edged closer to Robin. Robin looked around, hoping maybe someone he knew would come by. He'd been bullied enough to be able to pick up a bad tone in Tyrone's voice.

"Football's all right." Robin stalled.

"Damn right it's all right," Tyrone growled and got so close that Robin could see the single hairs of his soul patch. "You want us to have a good team. Right, Shrimp?"

"For sure, Tyrone," Robin answered quickly.

"Then you gonna help yo' boy Tyrone. Because if yo' boy Tyrone don' get good grades, he'll get his ass kicked off the team. Tyrone don't want that, so you gonna help yo' boy. And you gonna keep yo' big yap shut 'bout it. You finish yo' essay for English? On that *Bud-whatevah* book?"

Robin nodded. "Uh-huh."

"That good," Tyrone said, then glared at Robin. "That mean you can write one for yo' boy Tyrone. Give it to me 'fore English on Monday. And handwrite it. I don't got no computer. Okay, Shrimp?"

Robin was silent. Tyrone was asking him to cheat.

"You not sayin' no, is you, Shrimp?"

Robin saw Tyrone's big hands curl into fists. He knew what his answer had to be if he didn't want to get dogged.

"Okay."

"Okay be right," Tyrone confirmed. "Make it good. Not as good as yours, but good enough. You feelin' me?"

Crap. Robin didn't want to help Tyrone cheat, but he really didn't want to get his ass kicked either. He said what had to be said, even if he hated himself for saying it.

"Okay."

Chapter Three

Though it was barely nine o'clock on a Saturday morning, Miz Paige set a red plastic beach bucket full of her special fried shrimp in front of Robin, Sly, and Kaykay.

"Dig in," she commanded, then wiped her hands on the first of many towels she'd go through in the day. "First batch o' the day is the best batch o' the day."

Robin smiled at his grandmother. She wore white pants, sensible shoes, a white blouse, and her green apron. It was hard to believe she was turning sixty. Her rounded face had no lines, and her hair was thick under her chef's hat. But Robin knew his grandma's body was not her friend. She had diabetes. She had arthritis. She needed pills for her blood pressure. Some weeks, it seemed like she spent more time at the community clinic than in her kitchen.

"I'd love some!" Sly reached for a shrimp. He popped it in his mouth and chewed with a dreamy expression on his face. "Miz Paige, you make the best shrimp. And I just had me some breakfast."

"Why, thank you, Sylvester Thomas, you a gentleman and a scholar." Miz Paige eyed Kaykay suspiciously. "What about 'chu, girl? You still on that I-don't-eat-no-animals thang?"

Kaykay nodded. "Yup. And you should be too. It's called bein' kind to animals and bein' kind to the earth."

Miz Paige harrumphed. "Might be kind for the earth, but that don't make it kind to your stomach. Besides, you ever seen a shrimp brain?" She took a pen from her apron and put a dot on the white paper tablecloth. "Smaller than that. He don't even know he's bein' cooked." She gave Kaykay another sideways look. "I'll bring you some old celery sticks, Kaykay. Enjoy 'em."

Miz Paige started back toward the kitchen, but Robin stopped her. "Can we talk now about the Center, Gramma? It's really important."

"Okay. Jus' hold on a second."

Miz Paige turned down the music—she loved to play old soul and Motown—and slid into an empty chair.

The Shrimp Shack chairs were all mismatched, and the walls were covered in notes and cards from happy customers. Near the cash register were some photos of Robin's parents, who'd died when he—

No, Robin told himself. *Don't think on that. You can't do nothing about that. Think about the Center.*

It was the next morning; a hot and humid day that had everyone in shorts and T-shirts. Robin and his buds had gathered to plan what they might do to save the Center. Actually, they had a plan—they were going to do a sidewalk sale over at Garvey and Thirteenth Street of stuff they didn't need and give the money to Sarge. What they wanted to do this morning was get Miz Paige to help out too.

"Okay, shoot," Miz Paige told the kids. "Make it fast. Got a par-tay this afternoon. Fifty-five pounds of deep fried."

"Well," Robin began. "You know we're doing that sale thing today."

"That's right. It's a good idea," his grandmother agreed.

Robin shifted uneasily. He hated asking anyone for help. "Well, we were thinking … maybe there's a way for the Shrimp Shack to help out."

Miz Paige narrowed her eyes. "You want me to donate some shrimp?"

"That's not a bad idea," Kaykay said.

"I was actually thinking something else," Robin told her. "I was thinking maybe you could charge an extra dollar for orders this week. With the extra money to go to the Center."

"I love that idea!" Kaykay exclaimed. "I'm an artist. I'll make a sign. We can hand out flyers at the sidewalk sale, and—"

"Whoa, whoa!" Miz Paige held up one hand. "I ain't said yes, yet."

Sly put aside a shrimp tail. "Say yes, Miz Paige. Everyone's gotta do their bit."

"Sylvester Thomas, you sound just like your daddy the preacher man," Miz Paige told him.

"Is that a yes?" Sly pressed.

Miz Paige nodded. "I guess. How 'bout if I try it out to'morra after church? You kids make your sign. If it don't cut into my sales too much, I'll keep it goin' till Wednesday. She looked at Robin. "It's a fine idea, Robin. Your momma and daddy …."

Robin finished the sentence in his mind. He'd heard it from her so many times.

Your momma and daddy would be proud of you.

He had an answer in his mind, but he didn't dare say it.

Great, Gramma. But that won't bring them back.

It was three hours later. Robin, Sly, and Kaykay were at the plaza at Thirteenth and Garvey—really a small strip of asphalt with some benches and a couple of sickly ash trees. Though people were not really supposed to be selling stuff, the cops never bothered anyone here.

"Raising money to save the Center!"

Kaykay called out as people milled around, looking at what various folks were selling.

"Come save the Center!" Sly added. "Buy for a good cause!"

Robin had lugged over about fifty books in plastic bags. Sly, who lived with his family in a frame house on Seventeenth, had brought magic tricks, card decks, and video games he'd quit playing. Kaykay, who lived in the projects east of Garvey, had brought art supplies and some plants. She'd written up a bunch of flyers about the dollar-added thing that Miz Paige was willing to do. "Raising money to save the Center!" she called out again.

"Come save the Center!" Sly repeated "Buy for a good cause!"

Maybe it was the brutal heat. Maybe they had the wrong stuff to sell. Whatever the reason, few folks took flyers and no one bought anything. Finally, a couple of middle-aged people stopped by. They looked familiar to Robin, but he couldn't place them.

"Mr. and Mrs. Plunkett!" Sly introduced them around. They were from church. "Gonna buy something for a good cause?"

"The best cause," Robin added.

Mr. Plunkett was really short. His wife was even shorter. They didn't have far to go to bend down and check out a couple of Robin's old books. One was a novel by Maya Angelou. The other was some *Mad Libs* that Robin had never filled out.

"Yeah, we heard the old place needs a new roof. I'll take these," Mr. Plunkett said. "How much?"

"Buck a piece," Robin told him.

"That's not gonna pay for a new roof," Mrs. Plunkett declared.

"It's a start," Kaykay responded.

Mr. Plunkett handed over the money

and shook his head sadly. "There's so many causes and things that need money. The community clinic's fixin' to shut down too. The church day care needs swings. There's men back from Iraq who don't even have a roof over their heads. Everybody's sufferin'. And everyone's stretched so thin."

"Clyde Plunkett, you hush!" Mrs. Plunkett interrupted him. "These kids are tryin' their best." She smiled at Robin and Sly and lifted her sunglasses. "You keep doin' what you're doin'. The good Lord will give you a hand. You have a good day now."

"See you, Mrs. Plunkett!" Sly called as they walked away. "Thanks, Mr. Plunkett!" He put the two dollars in his pocket. "Two bucks down, twenty-four thou nine hundred ninety-eight to go."

Mr. Plunkett's words rang in Robin's head.

There's so many causes and things that need money. The community clinic's fixin' to shut down too. The church day care needs swings. There's men back from Iraq who don't even have a roof over their heads. Everybody's sufferin'. And everyone's stretched so thin.

By the time evening came, they'd made exactly seventeen dollars.

Robin trudged home carrying his unsold books and Kaykay's sign. When he got to the Shrimp Shack, his grandmother was starting to close. He taped the sign in the window, told her about the afternoon, and pitched in on cleanup. He could do it with his eyes closed.

Scrub the grill. Scrub the slicer. Scrub the floor. Scrub the tables. Scrub the grease catcher. Scrub the fridge. Scrub the sink. Scrub this, scrub that.

Does my gramma dream about shrimp and scrub brushes? Probably.

He took the trash—shrimp guts that stunk to high heaven—to the dumpster. This was always his last chore.

When he came back, he expected to find the lights half off and his grandmother ready to roll. Instead, he saw his grandmother face to face with a young man. He was in his early twenties, had a black bandana in his back pocket, and another around his head.

Ninth Street Ranger. Robin shivered. Those guys were badass.

"This be a bad block, an' I don't want nothin' to happen to yo' shop, Miz Paige," the guy was saying, all fake nice. "That'd be a bad thing, Miz Paige. You know what I'm sayin'?"

"I know just what you're sayin'!" Miz Paige exclaimed. "You're shakin' me down!

Get your scabby ass outta my shop! Get out!"

"You don't wan' to do that," the guy hissed. "You wanna give us a hundred bucks a week so nothin' bad happens."

His grandmother was furious. "I worked my life buildin' this business! You are not shakin' me down!"

The Ranger must have seen Robin out of the corner of his eye. He whirled. "Who you be? Whatchu want?"

"That's my grandson. You stay away from him!" Miz Paige exclaimed.

The Ranger laughed. "That's your grandson? I heard 'bout him." He took two threatening steps toward Robin. "I hear you a little smarty-pants. Tell you what, Smarty Pants. You wanna be smart? Tell your grams to do the right thing an' gimme the money. Or she gonna be very, very sorry!"

Chapter Four

It seemed like a regular late-August morning on Ninth Street as Robin and Miz Paige stepped outside to go to church. Robin took in a Ninth Street scene bathed in bright, warm sunshine. Regular Sunday. The Ninth Street Ranger lookouts were on both corners waiting for the white kids who drove in from the suburbs to buy drugs. Some folks were walking their dogs. The little liquor store that Mr. Burress ran just down from the Shrimp Shack was doing a brisk business in Lotto tickets.

Like any regular Sunday morning. Robin and Miz Paige were on their way to the ten o'clock service at Ironwood Baptist Church. Miz Paige was big on church, and big on taking Robin to church. She sang in the choir and always wore a long black skirt and a short-sleeve flower-print top. A choir robe went over all this. Robin wore what he called his regular church suit—a black jacket and pants, green collared shirt, and a black tie.

Robin was hot and cold on church. He liked it because Kaykay was always there. Sometimes, though, after a week with lots of gunshots and sirens? All he wanted to do on Sunday morning was sleep.

Robin and his grandmother stepped in front of the Shrimp Shack, and the regular morning stopped being regular.

"Robinson Paige, my word! Is that door ajar?"

Miz Paige stood on the sidewalk with hands on her hips and real concern in her voice. His grandmother only called him

"Robinson Paige" when something was wrong. He'd been named for the baseball great Jackie Robinson. His grandmother also claimed that the Hall of Fame pitcher Leroy "Satchel" Paige had actually been a distant relative.

Robin peered at the Shrimp Shack front door, which was behind a pull-down metal gate designed to keep out anyone who might even think about robbing them. *Oh no.* The door to the place was cracked open behind the gate.

"I think so, Gramma," Robin told her. "You locked it last night, right? And the gate?! Did you lock the gate?"

"Help me, Jesus," Miz Paige muttered as she opened the now unlocked gate. "Help me, help me, help me."

She rolled up the gate; the front door was definitely open. They opened it all the way and stepped inside.

"Sweet Jesus!" Miz Paige exclaimed. "Robinson Paige, call the police!"

Robin's heart beat harshly as he took out his cell and called 911. The Shrimp Shack was trashed. Tables upside down. Chairs broken. Cards and letters that had once been on the wall were now on the floor. Robin winced. Someone had found Miz Paige's giant jar of tartar sauce and hurled it against the photo of his dead parents. It was now covered in scuzzy, green-specked sauce.

"Hello?" he said when the 911 operator answered. "This is Robin Paige at the Shrimp Shack on Ninth Street. We got broken into last night. There's a lot of damage."

Miz Paige hustled over to look in her cash register. "They took 'zactly a hundred dollars!" she wailed.

The operator asked Robin if he and his grandmother were in any danger. When Robin said he didn't think so, the 911 lady said they'd send a patrol car over as soon as one got free.

"Call the church and tell Reverend Thomas what's goin' on," Miz Paige instructed when the call was over. Her voice was steadier. "Lemme check out the freezer and make sure there's no dead bodies."

"Why didn't the alarm go off?" he asked.

Miz Paige made a face. "Didn't pay the bill. Tryin' to save some money for your college."

That made Robin mad. "I don't go to college for four years! We live on a bad street! We got gang guys shakin' us down!" He was so upset his speech was turning street. "Come on, Gramma. Pay your damn alarm bill!"

Miz Paige just looked at him, then went to the back. Meanwhile, Robin called the church and told the choir director what had happened.

"Everything's still there," Miz Paige announced when she returned. "Strange."

"No it ain't." Robin had it figured out. "It's not strange. The Rangers are sending you a message. They took a hundred dollars. That's what they wanted you to pay them."

Miz Paige bit her lower lip, nodded, and looked up toward the sky. "God, forgive me for what I'm about to do." Then she stared hard at Robin. "We're gonna spruce this place up. And we're not gonna say a word to the po-lice."

"What?!"

"The cops'll take a report and leave," his grandmother told him. "Meanwhile, we gots to live here. No, Robin. You do not say a word. Do you understand?"

Robin understood. He didn't like it, but he understood. His grandmother was afraid of the Rangers like he was afraid of Tyrone.

"I understand."

Miz Paige managed a little smile. "Good. Now, you start in front, an' I'll start in back. This mess ain't gonna clean itself."

Robin couldn't help himself. He had to ask. "You gonna pay off the Rangers, Gramma?"

Her answer was lightning quick. "To keep you safe, Robin? I'll give them anything."

She went to the back. Robin took off his jacket and tie, rolled up his sleeves, and found the push broom. He'd just finished his first pass when he heard loud knocking on the front door.

He froze. Too quick to be the cops, he was sure it was the Rangers coming for their money. He steadied his hands as he opened the wooden door.

It wasn't the Rangers. It was Reverend Thomas. Right behind him were Sly and Kaykay, and behind them were a bunch of people in their Sunday best.

"Robin, Robin!" Reverend Thomas was a big man, and he had a booming, friendly voice. "We hear you had a little problem last night. We're here to help you clean this ungodly mess, and maybe I'll do a little preachin' when we're done. Sometimes the best place to have church is not in a church at all." He got a twinkle in his eye. "That is, if Miz Paige promises to cook up some of her real fine shrimp!"

Everyone laughed.

Then a voice rang out from behind Robin. His grandmother's.

"Praise the Lord and find yo'selves some paper towels," Miz Paige announced. "There's work to do … and then there'll be shrimp to eat!"

Just after nightfall, Robin leaned back against his pillows and thought about the strange day. The trashing of the Shrimp

Shack. What his grandmother had said about the Rangers. And especially the way two dozen people working together made the place look good as new in a couple of hours. Someone even managed to clean up the pictures of his parents.

Of course, the police weren't happy.

The cops had shown up around noon. They took a report and even asked questions at the liquor store. The owner, Mr. Burress, said he hadn't heard a thing. Whether that was true, or whether Mr. Burress was also afraid of the Rangers, Robin didn't know.

He got up from his bed, went to his single window, and looked out. Ninth Street was deserted except for the usual lookouts. His grandmother had gone to see a sick friend. He was home by himself. Tomorrow was the first real day of school. He had homework to do. Not for himself. For Tyrone.

Robin's room wasn't much. Just a single bed, a desk, a lamp, a chair, and a bookcase. But he had an old computer and printer that Miz Paige used to run her business. He knew he was lucky to have a computer. A lot of kids had to use the ones at the library or the Center. Tonight's homework, though, couldn't be done on the computer. It had to be handwritten.

Robin sighed, then found a binder and tore out some sheets of paper. Writing another essay about *Bud, Not Buddy* was a snap. It only took about forty-five minutes. He made sure to mess up some of the grammar and spell some words wrong so the teacher would believe it was Tyrone's. Then he put Tyrone's name and the date at the top.

I can't believe I'm doing this, Robin mused. *Actually? After today? I can believe it.*

The thought didn't make him feel any better. Not at all.

Chapter Five

Robin sat in the second row in English, not far from Sly and Kaykay. It was a big class—probably thirty-eight kids—and everyone was listening intently as Tyrone read the very end of his five paragraph essay about *Bud, Not Buddy*.

His essay, as in, my essay. As in, the one I wrote for him, Robin thought bitterly.

"In con-cluse—in conclusion," Tyrone read, having trouble with the word conclusion, which Robin had spelled the correctly. "*Bud, Not Buddy* is a fine novel about a boy who is searching for family. He was lucky that Lefty Lewis found him walking by the side of the road. By the end of the book, Bud Caldwell realizes that without a family, a person is not a whole person. We all need family. How we make our family is a big part of what it means to be human. The end."

Silence.

Robin looked around. His classmates stared at Tyrone in shock. Most everyone knew Tyrone, at least by rep. Tyrone always blew off his homework. That Tyrone Davis could write an essay like this was nothing but amazing.

The whole class broke into wild applause and cheering. Tyrone took an actual bow, and there was even more clapping, hooting, and hollering.

"You da man! Ty-rone!" Tyrone's homeboy, Riondo Moore, another football player who everyone just called "Dodo," shouted at his friend.

Tyrone encouraged the clapping. "Give it up fo' me!"

Aw, man. I have to clap for this?

Finally, Robin clapped so he wouldn't be the only kid not clapping. That was part of his school strategy. Stay under the radar. Do good on tests and reports. Go easy on the class participation. Don't attract too much attention.

You don't want to be "It." Not at Ironwood Central High School. This place is a jungle!

Robin knew all about being "It." He'd been "It" many times in grade school and middle school. He didn't need to be "It" again: to be picked on, beat on, and jacked up.

Not interested in that. As Sly would say, "No way, no how."

Tyrone pointed at Robin and grinned as the applause continued. Even the teacher,

Mr. Simesso joined in. Finally, he held a hand up for quiet.

Robin liked Mr. Simesso a lot. The orientation on Friday had been with him. He'd come to America from Ethiopia for college and stayed to be in the Teach for America program. This was his second year. He had a good rep, and the girls thought he was cute. About five eight, oval face, scruffy beard, glasses, and a cool Ethiopian accent.

"Nicely done, Tyrone," Mr. Simesso commented. "I know your teachers from last year. I can see that you're turning over a new leaf."

"Tryin' to," Tyrone responded. "Tryin' to make me some straight As."

Some of his boys in the back of the room cracked up, especially Dodo.

They must know he didn't write that paper.

"Whatever you did, Tyrone? Keep it up," Mr. Simesso advised. "Next assignment, class? Pick ten words you don't know from *Bud, Not Buddy*. Write out the word, the definition, and use the word in a sentence. Don't forget to note what page the word is on. Due Wednesday. Tyrone, you can sit down."

As Tyrone strutted back to his seat, Mr. Simesso turned to Robin. "Robin Paige, do you have anything to add to our discussion of *Bud, Not Buddy*?"

Robin hated to be called on. Too much attention.

He shook his head.

"Is that a no?" Mr. Simesso asked.

Robin nodded.

"Because you have an excellent academic reputation, Robin," Mr. Simesso went on.

Some guy in the back of the room called out, "Shrimp!"

Mr. Simesso whirled. "Who said that?"

Whoever it was, he was saved by the bell. The class streamed out. Robin's friends were waiting for him outside in the hall. On Monday, English was right before lunch, and they always ate lunch together. That is, if you could call what got served in the ICHS cafeteria "lunch." Robin had tried the food on orientation day. The fish sticks tasted like month-old shrimp guts.

"Okay," Kaykay declared as soon as Robin joined them. "No way Tyrone wrote that. He doesn't know any verbs other than 'to be.' If it's over two syllables, forget it."

"I was thinkin' the same thing," Sly agreed. "He be boastin' how he gonna make all As? No way, no how."

"Last A Tyrone made was in preschool," Kaykay sniffed. "And that was with the teacher's help!"

These are my friends, Robin mused. *I*

can't lie to them. If I don't tell the truth,
that's the same as lying.

"Umm … that essay? He didn't write
it." Robin said.

"How you know that?" Sly demanded.
"You got the four-one-one?"

Robin edged closer to the wall as the
tide of students heading to the cafeteria got
thick. To save money, the city had closed
a bunch of the other high schools, which
meant that Ironwood Central was jammed.

"Yes, I got straight dope. Tyrone didn't
write that essay." Robin's mouth felt dry. "I
did."

"You did what?" Kaykay was shocked.

"I wrote Tyrone's essay. 'Cause I didn't
want to get my ass kicked!"

"What happened, Robin? I got to know."
Sly was as upset as Kaykay.

Robin sighed. "Let's eat. I'll tell you
everything."

In the crowded, noisy cafeteria, the kids sat at the end near the teachers' lounge, far away from the jock table where Tyrone and his football buddies were hanging out. Robin and Sly got baloney sandwiches, milk, and bananas. Sly added a brownie. Kaykay always brought her lunch from home in a reusable "green" container. Today, it was bean spout salad, a small apple, and a few organic crackers.

"You eatin' hamster food," Sly told her after his first big bite of the sandwich.

"Not like two people I know," Kaykay retorted as she opened her salad. She looked at Robin. "You. Tyrone. Spill!"

Robin did. He told them everything, from what happened with Tyrone after leaving the Center on Friday to writing the essay for him last night.

When he was done, Sly drained his milk and shook his head. "You know when it start with a boy like Tyrone, it don't stop. You in for a bad year, Robin."

"Well, what do you want him to do?" Kaykay demanded. "You want him to get his butt whipped? Know what, Sly? Why don't you go over to Tyrone right now and tell him you gonna be his homework boy?"

Sly pursed his lips. "Kaykay, back yo' ass off. I get it. I don't like it, but I get it."

Kaykay nodded. "Damn straight you get it."

The kids ate silently for a few minutes. Not that it was ever quiet in the cafeteria. Lunch was in two shifts, six hundred kids each. ICHS was an old school, built decades ago, with six hundred kids eating in a cafeteria built for half that many. The mix of talking, laughing, and yelling was anything but quiet. Robin was so upset about how he'd helped Tyrone cheat that the noise felt like punches against his eardrums.

"I'll figure out something to do with Tyrone," he finally told his friends, hoping his voice had more courage than he felt. "Meanwhile, what are we going to do about the Center? My grandmother made about a hundred extra dollars on shrimp yesterday afternoon. That ain't gonna be enough."

Sly swallowed down a bite of the sandwich. "Maybe it'll be better today."

"Maybe," Robin allowed. He didn't feel confident.

"If only there's a way to get everyone to give a dollar, not just folks buying shrimp," Kaykay said, then closed up her container so she could use it again.

Robin got a faraway look in his eyes. He had an idea. It might even be a good idea.

"Know what, dudes?" he asked his buds. "Maybe there is."

Four hours later, Robin, Kaykay, and

Sly had Miz Paige surrounded in the Shrimp Shack.

"I just gave you kids a hundred dollars I made for the Center!" she declared. She loosened her apron. "Now you kids want to sell raffle tickets?"

"A hundred bucks ain't gonna put no new roof on the Center," Sly told her.

"We need more money," Kaykay insisted. "Lots more."

Robin looked right at his grandmother. "We stopped at the Center on the way home and talked to Sarge. There's just two days left, and they've only raised about two thousand bucks. So we were thinking, we go out and sell raffle tickets for five dollars. Each ticket gives the buyer a chance to win a fifty dollar dinner here at the Shrimp Shack. Who wouldn't take that chance?"

Miz Paige frowned. " 'Bout a million folks I know."

"Can we try it, Gramma?' Robin asked.

"I'll think about it," was all Miz Paige would say. "Okay, you kids go on now. I need to talk to Robin."

His friends took off. As soon as they were gone, his grandmother handed Robin a sealed yellow envelope. He got a sinking feeling in his stomach. He knew what this was about.

"Hard to talk about free dinners when I'm givin' money away. You know where the Ninth Street Rangers hang out?" she asked.

Robin nodded.

"Take this to 'em. Tell 'em it's from me," she said softly. "Tell 'em there'll be the same every week; just please leave my shop alone. You understand me, Robin Paige?"

Robin nodded again. "Yes, Gramma."

"You understand why I'm doin' this? You play with fire, you get yo'self burned. I don't want us to get burned again. We been burned enough, don'chu think?"

Robin understood very well. But that yellow envelope he was holding and the reason he was holding it still made him mad as hell.

Chapter Six

Robin did know where the Rangers hung out. At both of ends of Ninth Street—at the intersection with Marcus Garvey Boulevard or the cross with Conyers Avenue—there were Rangers' drug lookouts on duty 24/7. Their faces changed with their shifts, but they all had black bandanas in their back pockets.

Robin had seen them in action many times. These were the new dudes in the gang, and their job was to flag down people looking to buy drugs. If it was a quick deal, they'd do it themselves. If it was major, they'd call in a big guy from the gang by cell phone.

I don't know why the cops don't bust these guys, Robin wondered as he headed for the intersection of Ninth and Garvey. On their side of the street was a Laundromat, Mr. Burress's liquor store, and the Shrimp Shack, plus a few squat apartment buildings. Across the street was the junk shop, a used CD place, and more apartment buildings. There were plenty of empty storefronts and plenty of empty apartments. No one wanted to live on Ninth if they could live someplace else. It was a bad block.

Maybe the cops know that if they bust those dudes, there'll be new Rangers the next day. Or maybe there's no more room in the jails. Or maybe the Rangers pay off the cops, like I'm about to pay them off. I don't know.

There was a short, stocky Ranger look-out on the far corner. He wore black pants and a white undershirt.

"Yo." Robin said, turning on his street voice as he approached him.

"Wassup, little man, you buyin'?" The guy barely moved his lips.

Robin shook his head no, angry that the lookout would be happy to sell drugs to a ninth-grader. "Nah, man. Jus' lookin' for a dude who stopped in the Shrimp Shack th' other night to talk wit' my ol' lady."

The lookout smiled, flashing four gold front teeth. "You from the Shrimp Shack? Word is you had a little trouble yesterday."

Robin shrugged. "When I talk wit' yo' boy, it won't happen no mo'. You know 'im?"

The guy looked at Robin closely. "What's yo' name?"

"Robin. Jus' say Smarty Pants be here."

The guy took out a cell—a nice one, Robin saw—and turned away to make a quick call.

A moment later, he turned back. "You wait. He be comin'."

"What's yo' name?" Robin asked boldly. He knew if he was going to be making pay-offs to the Rangers, he needed a little street cred.

"My name be for me to know and you not to find out. Go round the corner on Garvey. My boy be comin'. He'll find you."

The convo was over. Robin went around the corner to Garvey. It was close to sunset, and the streets were getting quiet again. It made him nervous to wait out there with an envelope full of money, but wait he did. Five minutes. Ten minutes. Then fifteen minutes.

Finally, a tricked-out black Mustang pulled over to the curb near him. The tinted window on the passenger side came down. Inside was the same Ranger who'd come to the Shrimp Shack the night before it got trashed. Robin could see he had a shaved head. There was another Ranger driving. That guy wore a sideways Chicago White Sox cap.

"Get in," the leader told Robin.

"No way," Robin said.

The Ranger smiled coldly. "I said get yo' ass in the car, Smarty Pants. What is it they call you at school? Shrimp? Shrimp, I said, get in!"

Robin panicked. The guy had learned his nickname.

What else does he know about me? Who my friends are? Where they live? Who goes to our church? When my grandmother puts her money in the bank?

Robin got in the Mustang.

"You smart, Shrimp," the Ranger grunted. He swung around to face Robin. Robin tried to memorize his face. There was a black mole under the guy's right nostril. "You very smart. But you not be here to teach me bi-ol-ogy. You got somethin' fo' me?"

"Word," Robin said.

He handed over the envelope. The guy barely glanced inside it before he started talking again. "Okay. Hundred a week, cash. Jus' like this. You do the drop; you too skinny to be packin', not like your grams!"

The driver cracked up. Robin gritted his teeth. Making fun of Miz Paige's weight— that was low.

The gang guy wasn't done. "Like I said, hundred a week, and yo' grams can sell all the shrimps she want. Hell, my boys and me, we might try some fo' ourselves!" The Ranger laughed; his driver joined in.

Robin hated them so much right then.

"Get yo' sorry smarty-pants ass out the car, Shrimp. See yo' sorry face next week," the Ranger spat. "You know how to find me. And you *betta* be lookin' fo' me, Shrimp."

Robin stepped out. The Mustang pulled away. Robin felt his knees actually bang together. That's how upset he was. Then his upset turned to anger.

How dare those guys! How dare they!

He started back toward the Shrimp Shack. He'd just passed the Rangers lookout when he heard his named called from behind him.

"Yo! Yo, Shrimp! We want to talk to you!"

Crap. He knew that voice. Tyrone.

Robin turned around. It was Tyrone. With him was Dodo Moore. Dodo was even bigger than Tyrone. Dodo and Tyrone were all sweaty. They wore ICHS football jerseys; Robin realized they must have come right from practice.

What are they doing on Ninth Street?

Robin got the answer to that question soon enough.

"Hey, Tyrone. Hey, Dodo," he muttered.

"Hey yo'self, Shrimp," Tyrone said. "Whatchu think of my essay today? I'm a born-again schol-ar! Be a schol-ar, get a dollar!"

He cracked up at his own stupid joke. Dodo cracked up too.

"We ain't got much time," Tyrone went on. "So, Shrimp. That vocab thing for Simesso? The one due day after to'morra? Do one for us too."

Here we go again, Robin moaned to himself. *I don't want to do their homework for them!*

He got an idea. Maybe, just maybe, they would go for it.

"How 'bout if you guys and me, we work on it together?" he offered. "I'll help you. Then it'd really be your homework. No harm in gettin' help."

"What a good idea!" Dodo exclaimed.

"How 'bout if maybe we bust your lame-ass face?"

"You gots two choices, Shrimp." Tyrone balled his big fists again. "Do one fo' us, or do one fo' us."

Robin tried to think of some way out of this. There wasn't one.

"Aight," he finally said. "English be first period Wednesday. I'll give it to you before."

"He a smart shrimp," Dodo told Tyrone. "But he still a shrimp."

"Yup. If he don' mess it up! If he mess it up? We make him shrimp cocktail an' eat him fo' lunch! Oh! One mo' thing."

Tyrone was carrying some school stuff. He handed Robin a stapled-together bunch of papers. Robin looked at it. On the front it read, TYRONE DAVIS, SCIENCE 9, TERM PAPER RUBRIC.

"You gonna do this paper for me," Tyrone stated. "Eight pages. Due in November."

"I'm not even in that class!" Robin protested.

"Ain't my problem. See you, Shrimp!"

The guys took off, giving each other fist bumps and high fives.

Robin trudged home. He checked in at the Shrimp Shack, where his grandmother told him she'd close up by herself if he wanted to go up to his room and read. That's what he did, but even though he had a great book—*Monster*, by Walter Dean Myers, about a good kid who got accused as an accessory in a murder—he couldn't focus. He went to the window and sat with his nose against the grimy glass, watching night fall on Ninth Street. Night was when the block got dicey. His grandmother didn't want him out after dark, and definitely not alone.

He sat and thought about Tyrone and Dodo. About giving the money to the Rangers. About how the Center was going down because there were too many good causes that needed help and not enough money to save them all. About—

Whoa.

Robin noticed something out on the street. Something strange.

Across the street was an apartment building right next to the junk shop. Below ground level was a place where everyone put their full garbage bags.

Robin saw someone down there, lit only by a streetlight, moving garbage bags around. He squinted, trying to get a better look.

Whoa. It's the drug lookout from before. I'm sure it's him. What the hell is he doing?

As Robin watched, the lookout moved a few more bags, then dropped to his knees. Robin's eyes followed him like a laser. He saw the lookout lift something off the ground. Robin couldn't see clearly, but it seemed like a flat paver stone.

The lookout put the paver stone to one side, took something out of his pocket, and whatever he took out he put down in the hole where the paver stone had been. Then he replaced the paver. Finally, he moved the garbage bags back where they'd been before. After a double-check to be sure he hadn't been seen, the lookout trotted back toward Garvey.

What the hell?

If he hadn't just paid off the Rangers, or if Tyrone and Dodo hadn't hit on him to do their schoolwork, he never would have done what he was about to do.

Whatever that dude was doing? I'm gonna find out!

Chapter Seven

It was totally against his grandmother's rules for Robin to go out alone after dark.

He did it anyway.

First, though, he prepared himself.

He put on black pants, a black shirt, and a black hoodie so that he might blend in with the night. He didn't wear shoes, just socks, so there'd be no footfalls on the street. He locked the apartment door behind him and made sure the building door was locked when he went out into the night.

His heart pounded as he looked both ways. He was not supposed to be doing this. The dealers were at either end of Ninth Street. No traffic. No one on foot. He darted across the street, heading for the landing where he'd seen the lookout do his thing.

Is this the most dumb-ass thing I've ever done? If that dude comes back, I'm dead!

He stepped down below street level to the flat area with the garbage bags. It stunk of stale beer and vomit. Before he started moving garbage bags, he checked to see if he was being watched. He wasn't. So he quietly started moving the bags, hoping to uncover the same loose stone the lookout had moved.

He breathed heavily. The bags were noisy. They stunk in his hands so much he almost barfed. He winced as he picked up one really heavy bag full of cans and bottles that rattled like a passing train. He was sure the lookouts would hear that.

Somehow, they didn't.

Finally, he'd moved all the bags. He wiped the sweat from his forehead and tried to figure out which paving stone was the loose one. He dropped to his knees and dug at the edges of one of the pavers. It didn't budge.

Another. Another. And another, and another, and another.

It wasn't until his fingers were raw and he was about to give up that one actually moved.

Omigod. This is it!

The paver under his fingers turned out to be a fake, made to look like the others. It didn't weigh more than a tray of shrimp. Robin lifted it with ease.

No time to waste now. If the lookout came back, he wasn't just dead. He was double-dead.

Heart racing, breath shallow, he reached into the hole the fake paver had covered. It was so dark that he couldn't really see, so he rooted around blindly until—

Yes!

An envelope! A thick envelope!

What's in it? Vials of crack? Smack? Money? All of the above?

He grabbed the envelope and shoved it in his waistband. Now he had to get out of there. Someone in the building could hear him. His grandmother could come home and find him missing. The lookout could come back. Both lookouts could come!

For a brief instant, Robin thought about tossing the envelope back in the hole, putting back the fake paver, tossing some garbage bags over the paver, and running home. That was the smart thing to do.

But no. He'd come this far. He hated the Rangers so much, and this envelope had to belong to them. So he replaced the fake paver and moved all the disgusting garbage bags back. His body was sweaty from effort and fear. His fingertips were bleeding. He knew he looked a mess. How would he ever explain himself if he was caught?

See it through, he told himself. *See it through. Then get your ass home.*

He did. Or at least he tried to.

His work done, he bounded up the steps to Ninth Street, thinking of what he'd do if the envelope was full of drugs. It would feel so damn good to flush those mothers down the toilet or open his window and scatter them to the wind. Maybe he'd make a little stack out of the glassine bags and burn them. How great would it be to watch thousands of dollars of gang drugs go up in flames instead of into people's lungs and veins?

Man, that would feel good.

He crouched at the top of the steps and looked both ways. The lookouts were busy dealing with customers. Robin could see their bodies hard against cars that had pulled up, headlights turned off. If there ever was a perfect time for him to cross, this was it.

He ran. He nearly fell when his stocking foot landed in a pothole left over from winter, but he kept his balance and kept running.

Get home.

Get inside.

Get upstairs.

Get the hell out of these clothes.

Get into a shower.

A scabby cat spotted him as he neared the building door. Frightened, it screamed like it had just been stabbed.

Damn! Shut up, cat!

The cat kept screaming. It was exactly the kind of thing that would bring the attention that Robin didn't want.

Gotta get inside, Robin thought frantically as he reached the door of his building and
fumbled for his key. *Gotta get in before—*

Too late.

"Hey! Stop!" a furious voice called
from behind him. "Hey! Who you be, an'
whatchu think you doin'?"

Chapter Eight

Hey!" the angry voice repeated. "Turn yo' ass around!"

In the split second before he turned around to face whoever had busted him, Robin thought about the best way to die.

Was it better to have your head blown off by a Glock? Robin figured that's what would happen when the lookout realized Robin had stolen his stash.

Or was it better to be dragged off to Ninth Street Rangers' headquarters and get beaten to a pulp, then tossed off an overpass onto the highway and get run over so many

times people couldn't tell if he'd been human or a lost dog?

Maybe they'd knife him. Beat him with
tire irons. Or make him pull the trigger in a
drive-by, then shoot him.

There were so many bad ways to die.

In the same split second he tried to think
of a reason he had the envelope in his waistband, no shoes on his feet, and why he was
sweaty and stinky.

There was no good reason.

I am so—

"I said, turn your ass around!" the voice
boomed.

No choice. Robin turned around.

It wasn't an angry Ranger lookout with
a Glock pointed at him.

It was his own grandmother. She held a
baseball bat in her right hand.

"Gramma?" Robin croaked.

"Robin Paige! Is that you in that black

hoodie?" Miz Paige strode over to him. "Why you out here? Why you all sweaty? Why you have no shoes on? What is goin' on?"

Robin felt sick, ashamed, and relieved all at once. He pulled down the black shirt so there was no way the envelope would show and tried to say something believable.

"Gramma, I … I …"

"Speak up, Robinson Paige! 'Fore I send you to yo' room for the rest of yo' life!"

"I … I …"

What to say? What to say? What to—I got it!

"Gramma, I heard a kitten!"

"You heard what?!"

"I heard a kitten!

Robin thought Miz Paige was going to unload the baseball bat on his behind. But then his grandmother seemed to realize they were still out on the street. She moved Robin aside, got out her own keys, and opened the building door. Then, under the harsh lighting of the yellow hallway, she lit into him again.

"You done heard a kitten! We live on the worst block in the city, and you go outside in your stocking feets 'cause you done heard a kitten! Who you think you be, Robin Paige? Doctor D-o-o-little?"

Robin had a vague idea of who Doctor Dolittle was—some guy from an old Eddie Murphy movie who could talk to animals. He was in deep now. He hated to lie to his grandma, but he had to make the kitten story sound real.

"It's true! I was up in my room readin', an' the window was open, an' I heard this kitten on the street. It sounded so sad. Then I heard the momma cat screechin'. The kitten was cryin', and it was breakin' my heart. I went to the window, and they were both in the middle of the street. Then a car came. Momma cat ran one way, and the kitten ran the other. Then the mother cat couldn't find the kitten and was wailin' up a storm. So I decided to go out and try to bring the kitten back to the momma."

Miz Paige frowned and wrinkled her forehead but didn't say anything.

She don't believe me, Robin thought frantically. *She don't believe me. If she don't believe me, what's she gonna do? Search me? Please, Gramma. Please! Don't search me!*

Robin decided the best thing to do was to confess.

"Gramma, the truth is, I—"

Miz Paige cut him off. "You a good person, Robin. Your daddy—my son—was a good person too. Like you. Maybe too good. Come to think of it, I heard that cat screechin' too."

"You did?" Robin couldn't believe he might get out of this alive.

His grandmother nodded. "Uh-huh. But next time you hear a lil' kitten in the street after dark? Call me. Call the animal shelter. Call anyone. Jus' don't go out there by yo'self!"

Omigod. She believes me. Now say the two most important words in the whole English language.

"Okay, Gramma."

"Okay. Hey! How come your fingers all bleedin'?" Miz Paige pointed the thick end of the baseball bat at Robin's right hand.

"Uh … "

"Robin?"

"Well … I was chasin' the kitten, an' it scratched me!" Robin knew that was lame.

"Did you bring it back to its momma?" Miz Paige asked.

Robin shook his head. "After it cut my finger, it ran away. Or something."

Once again, he felt her on the verge of not believing him. Who could blame her? His story was so lame-ass.

But Miz Paige believed him.

"Okay, Robin. Let's go up," she said. "Take a shower and get to bed. And if you ever go out like that again? I've never hit you. Not one time since your momma and daddy passed on. But if you do this again? I'm gonna tan your hide, and no one's gonna blame me!"

Safe. I'm safe!

His grandmother embraced him. He hugged her back, but he was careful not to let her feel the envelope still tucked into his waistband.

A few moments later, Robin was letting them into the apartment.

The apartment was small, but it had everything they needed. Robin sometimes wondered what rich folks did with all the empty rooms in their mansions. If you had a family of four, did you really need seven bedrooms?

There was his little bedroom, a slightly bigger one for his grandmother, and one bathroom with a decent shower. There was a small kitchen with an electric stove, a fridge, and a microwave that only worked sometimes, but no dishwasher. There was also a combo living room and dining room. It had an old-style twenty-inch TV and furniture as mismatched as the chairs in the Shrimp Shack. No air conditioner. Even though their place faced north, when it got blazing hot, they suffered.

There was one thing in the place Robin loved. The bookcase in his room. They had a big one, which they'd lugged home together from a sale on Thirteenth Street a few years ago. Like Robin, Miz Paige loved books. She sometimes even took payment at the Shrimp Shack in books if folks had no money. Not that she has time to read.

Robin headed down the hall toward the bathroom, the envelope still tucked safely in his waistband. There were a few framed photos on the walls: pictures of President Obama, President Kennedy, and Dr. Martin Luther King. Also some family shots. Robin had cousins, aunts, and uncles on the West Coast and in South Carolina. He didn't see them much, but when he did, it was stupid fun.

There was a single framed photo of his parents, Randolph and Nicole Paige. It had been taken on their honeymoon in Mexico, three years before their car slid off the road in a snowstorm and into the big lake. They seemed so mismatched in their swimsuits on the beach—his dad tall and thin, his mom short and round. But they had their arms around each other like they never wanted to let go.

Robin's heart ached as he gazed at the picture. He loved his grandmother, but he never really got to know his parents. That felt wrong. Sometimes he'd stand in front of this photograph and talk to his parents in his head.

He talked to them now.

"What do you think of what I did tonight, Dad? What do you think, Mom? Do you think I have guts, or do you think I'm being stupid? How does a person know which is which?"

No answer. Just his parents' happy faces frozen forever behind a glass frame, with no clue how it would end.

Robin felt a lump rise in his throat and forced himself away. He made a quick pit stop in his room for clean shorts and a white muscle T-shirt—not that he had any muscles—and then went into the bathroom. He locked the door and started the shower to cover any sounds he might make.

His heart thudded when he took the envelope from his waistband. It was thick, yellow, and bigger than a regular envelope. It had a metal clasp. Whatever was in there? It was more than just paper.

He undid the clasp, then dumped the envelope upside down in the sink.

Whoa.

Dozens of glassine bags of drugs dropped into the yellowing porcelain.

And cash. Lots and lots of folded and wadded-up cash.

Robin quickly gathered the drug containers, dumped them in the toilet, and flushed twice. Ten seconds later, they were gone. He had no idea if it was smack or crack, but it had to be worth thousands. Then he counted the money, making messy piles of twenties, fifties, and hundreds on top of the toilet seat. It was more money than he'd ever seen in his life.

Holy moly. He counted again, and again, unable to believe the total he was keeping in his head.

The last two counts matched up.

"Twenty-five thousand three hundred bucks," Robin muttered. "That's a lotta chip."

He put it back into the envelope, double-checked the door lock, and stepped into the shower. He had a lot of thinking to do. There was no better time than right now to start doing it.

Chapter Nine

How much money you jus' say?" Sly asked.

"Twenty-five thou," Robin whispered. He didn't dare let anyone hear him. It was tricky enough to be talking in semi-public with Kaykay and Sly, but his best friends had to be told. "Actually, twenty-five thousand three hundred."

"You're kiddin', man." Sly clomped him on the back. "That is a good story, dude. You totally had us! He have you, Kaykay?"

Kaykay nodded. "Big time! Robin, you funny!"

It was the next morning. Robin was at free breakfast in the ICHS cafeteria, along with about half the school. Kaykay got free breakfast too. Her dad was a machinist who'd been out of a job for two years, and her mom was a nurse's aide. They had a big family, which meant she ate a lot of ninety-niners. That is, meals right from the ninety-nine-cent store. Sly wasn't eligible for free breakfast, but he came and hung out anyway.

Before Robin left for school that morning, he'd wanted to hide the money, but he couldn't find a really safe place. His grandmother got on these crazy cleaning jags; one could strike without warning. Finally, he tucked the money-stuffed envelope back in his waistband, under his school uni shirt. He hoped that he didn't look too puffy. But he had an answer for that: too much spaghetti for dinner. He didn't have gym that day, so he felt safe.

Sort of.

Once again, Robin was whipped. It had

been impossible to sleep. All this money! There were so many things that he and his grandmother needed. New furniture. A decent TV. They both needed new shoes. Plus, there was a ton of stuff they could do to fix up the Shrimp Shack.

The best part of the night had been when he realized that he could pay off the Ninth Street Rangers with money he'd stolen from them.

That made Robin feel great. Powerful, even.

Robin shook his head. "No story, dudes. I'm serious as a heart attack."

"Where the money be now?" Kaykay demanded. She wiped some juice from her mouth with a napkin and then polished up an apple. Even at free breakfast, she only ate and drank the natural stuff.

Robin tapped his waistband. "Right here."

"What?" Sly exclaimed.

"You be careful, Robin," Kaykay advised. "You be super careful. Those Rangers find out it's you, they gonna jack you up and jack up yo' grams."

Sly couldn't contain himself. He cackled. "Day-um, Robin. You rich!"

"Sssh, Sly!" Kaykay warned.

Robin thought it was best to end this convo. "I'm getting more milk, dudes," he said, pushing back from the table.

"You do that," Sly told him. "Me 'n Kaykay gonna figure out the best way to invest that chip. I'm gonna turn twenty-five thou into a hundred big ones, like that!" He snapped his fingers as if to show it would be a breeze.

Robin shook his head and went back to the food line. Before he knew it, Tyrone and Dodo had slipped into the line behind him. Robin bit his lower lip. What if those guys roughed him up and the envelope fell out?

What if they knew guys in the Rangers and knew about the money being stolen? They'd be heroes to the Rangers, and he'd be the dead dude walkin'.

"Wassup, Shrimp!" Dodo put a meaty hand on Robin's shoulder.

"Hey, Dodo."

"How be our homework?" Tyrone demanded.

"I'm … I'm gonna do it tonight," Robin said. That was the truth.

"Don't mess up, Shrimp," was Tyrone's response. "You don't want the whole football team mad at chu. Jus' be our beeyotch, and you be fine, Shrimp. "

He and Dodo moved off. Robin breathed a little easier, even though it hurt to be called a beeyotch. What had happened last night had made Robin determined. Yes, he'd do their homework tonight, but there was no way he'd do it forever.

Robin Paige was not going to be any-body's beeyotch.

Not only that, he'd just figured out what to do with the money.

"Be cool," Robin warned his friends as they entered the Center after school.

"You runnin' this show, Robin," Sly told him.

"Actually, you're doing the show," Robin reminded him. "You keep everybody's eyes on you."

"It won't take Robin and me more than two minutes," Kaykay promised. "Maybe less."

"Yo, Kaykay. I've got tricks that take longer than two minutes. Anytime you wanna be my assistant, you get five percent of whatever I make," Sly told her.

"Sly, you crazy! I ain't never gonna be no one's assistant," Kaykay declared.

"Dudes, shut up," Robin ordered as they entered the rec room. "Go set up, Sly. Kaykay, go with him. Start the show in five minutes."

The rec hall was full of people, quiet as a funeral parlor. Tomorrow was closing day, and there was supposed to be a party to celebrate the Center's long life. There was even a theme for the party: All Things Must End.

It didn't seem like many people were getting in the mood to party, though. Everyone was moving like ghosts, even as they put up decorations. Robin saw Mr. Smith taping crepe paper around a door. He joined him, and they worked silently.

"I'm gonna miss you, Robin," Mr. Smith finally said.

"I'm gonna miss you too, Mr. Smith," Robin replied.

"You won't forget me?"

Robin looked Mr. Smith in the eye. "I'll never forget you."

Suddenly, Kaykay's voice rang out from the stage. "Come one, come all! For a very special magic show by our own Mister Magic, Sly Thomas! In honor of all the good times you've had at the Center. Come on, peeps. Put down your stuff and have some fun!"

Everyone loved Sly's magic, so the stage area got crowded. Sly kept a trunk of magic props at the back of the stage, so he had all his gear. Kaykay joined Robin as Sly started his first trick by bringing a really old lady named Mrs. Leland on stage. She was almost ninety. He flirted with her, and she flirted right back, which made everyone laugh. Then Sly swallowed what seemed like a hundred needles and had Mrs. Leland look in his mouth with a flashlight.

"No needles in this big boy!" Mrs. Leland

yelled to the crowd. Worries forgotten for a moment, everyone cracked up.

"As they say in Paris," Sly responded, "You wrong!"

He opened his mouth, took hold of a thread that had magically appeared, and tugged it. Out came the thread. On the thread were strung the hundred needles. Everyone cheered and clapped. It was an amazing trick.

As Sly started his next trick, which involved a huge black top hat, Robin leaned close to Kaykay.

"This is a long trick. Let's do it," he whispered.

With the crowd distracted by Sly, he and Kaykay slipped out of the rec room. Once they hit the main hallway, they ran to the back offices and stopped outside Sarge's door.

"Ready?" Robin asked.

Kaykay nodded.

Robin handed the cash-filled envelope to her. She dug out a black Sharpie pen and quickly drew a pretty Christmas tree on the back of the envelope. Then she wrote some words in plain block capital letters.

MERRY EARLY XMAS
TO THE CENTER !

Work done, she gave the envelope back to Robin. "It's your money. You do it."

Robin didn't waste a second. He dropped to his knees and slipped the envelope through the big crack under Sarge's door. The moment the envelope was out of sight, he and Kaykay ran back to the rec hall. They got back in time to see Sly take a glass of water from the top hat, pour the water into the hat, and then put the hat on his head.

No water ran out. The crowd loved it.

Kaykay leaned toward Robin. "When do you think Sarge is going to—"

Just then Sarge came running into the rec room, bellowing. "We're saved! We're saved! Oh my word, oh my word, we're saved!"

As everyone watched in shock, he did a front flip, two cartwheels, and then another front flip, yelling all the while. "We're saved! We're saved!"

People stared like he'd lost his mind.

That's when Sarge opened the envelope that he'd stuffed in the pocket of his red warm-up suit. "Money! Enough to save the Center! Money! Someone just put it under my door. Money!" He flung a fistful of bills toward the ceiling. They fluttered down like dancing butterflies. "Money!"

Now, people understood. The place erupted in joyful shouting and cheers. Some of the old people were actually crying.

Sly came down from the stage to join Robin and Kaykay. Robin bumped his fist but said nothing. They'd talked about this: they didn't want to give anyone the idea that they were involved. In fact, they started dancing as happily as anyone.

That's when Mr. Smith creaked over to them. He was grinning from ear to ear.

"The Center's saved!" Robin punched the air with happiness.

"It's great!" Sly added. He did a few cool pops.

"Greater 'n great!" Kaykay yelled. "Woot! Woot!"

"Oh yeah, it's great all right." Mr. Smith said, but the smile left his face. "Bein' old ain't great. Bein' old means I can't run, and it means I need glasses to read, but it don't mean I can't see. Right, Robin? Right, Kaykay?"

Mr. Smith took Robin—who could tell something was terribly wrong—by the shoulders and spun him with surprising force, then got right in his face. "I may be old, an' I may move slow, but that don't mean I don't got eyes that can't see good as ever. Robin and Kaykay? I saw you two put an envelope under Sarge's door! Now, 'fess up!"

Chapter Ten

Robin just stood there, feeling horrible and trapped. His friends were silent. Sly was studying the stained ceiling of the rec hall. Kaykay's eyes were focused on the chipped tile floor like it had the word of God Almighty written in real gold.

"Robin?" Mr. Smith's hands tightened. "I may be 'bout eighty years old, but I will not stand for bull—you know what I mean. Now 'fess up to how you got yo' hands on that money, or I'll call Sarge, Miz Paige, Reverend Thomas, and Kaykay's parents, and maybe the Ironwood po-lice ... and you can 'fess up to all o' them!"

Robin ran possible excuses through his head. Could he say he'd found the money on the street? Could he claim Miz Paige had given it to him?

No. Those were beat excuses. Worse than beat. Stupid-ass, lame-ass, and beat. Also, they were lies. He hated to lie. He still felt bad about lying to his grandmother.

Just past Mr. Smith was one of the small meeting rooms. Everyone in the rec hall was still dancing around, thrilled by Sarge's amazing announcement.

No one's gonna miss us if we dip for a few.

"Come on," he told Mr. Smith. "We need to talk."

The meeting room was smallish, containing just folding chairs and a whiteboard. The fluorescent lights hummed and flickered. With the door closed, the celebration outside was muffled.

Mr. Smith blocked the door. "Till I hear the truth, no one's leavin'."

Robin breathed. The air in the room stank of sour coffee, stale doughnuts, moldy pizza, old lady perfume, and old man sweat. It made Robin want to retch. Or maybe it was just fear of what Mr. Smith would do when he heard the truth.

"Talk, son!" Mr. Smith ordered.

Robin talked.

He started all the way back in grade school, when Tyrone Davis had first called him Shrimp. He confessed how Tyrone and Dodo were shaking him down for homework the same way the Ninth Street Rangers shook down the Shrimp Shack. He talked about how he felt when the Shrimp Shack got trashed. He explained how he, Sly, and Kaykay tried to raise money to save the Center, but how it was impossible.

He told how weak he felt when he'd

paid protection money to the Rangers, and how angry he was when he saw the Ranger drug lookout through his window, hiding something across the street.

"I can't 'zactly explain it, Mr. Smith," Robin said softly. "It was like somethin' or someone tellin' me, 'Robin Paige, this be your moment. You can either let it go or take it.' "

He looked at his friends somberly and then at Mr. Smith. "I took it."

"You sure did," Mr. Smith responded. "You done took a chance, and you done took a gang's money. You know what they gonna do when they find out?"

Robin nodded grimly. "That can't happen."

Mr. Smith rocked a little from side to side. "Leastways you did one smart thing. Givin' it here 'stead of spending it all over the neighborhood." He turned to Sly and Kaykay. "Whatchu kids think of all this?"

Kaykay spoke with her usual bluntness. "What Robin did with the money is dope. Tyrone and Dodo's homework? Reverse dope."

Mr. Smith looked at Sly. "What about you? Wouldn't your daddy, the preacher man, say your boy, Robin, is a thief? That stealin' is a sin? An' that he helped your two classmates steal, in a way?"

Robin saw Sly bristle. "Mr. Smith, you old. I ain't afraid to say that. You don't know how it be out there. What Tyrone and Dodo be doin', makin' Robin do their homework? What the Rangers be doin', tellin' Robin's grandma to pay them off and then wreckin' her shop when she don't? Sellin' drugs on every corner? Messin' up the hood? They be the sinners! Not Robin! That's what my daddy would preach about!"

Wow. That was amazing. Sly sounded just like his daddy!

Mr. Smith rubbed the bristle on his chin with his right hand and then checked to make sure the door was tightly closed. In fact, he locked it.

"Don't want no one comin' in for what I gotta say," he explained. "You kids, sit. My legs be weary."

Mr. Smith ambled to a folding chair and put himself in it ass-backward, resting his thin arms on the back of the chair. Robin and the other kids got chairs near him.

"Would you do it again, Robin?" Mr. Smith suddenly asked.

The question took Robin by surprise. " 'Scuse me?"

Mr. Smith raised his thin eyebrows. "It's not a tough question. Would you do it again?"

"You mean, take money from the bad guys like the Rangers to save a place like the Center?" Robin fired back. "Fo' sho',

Mr. Smith. I'd do it a hundred times! I hope I get a chance to do it all over again!"

Mr. Smith chuckled lightly. "Well then. Looks like you making yo'self out to be a regular Robin Hood. Stealin' from the rich, an' givin' to the poor."

Robin hesitated. "You're not gonna get me in trouble?

Mr. Smith stood and balanced on his cane. "Here's what I gotta say. I been in this hood a long time. I 'member what it was, and I know what it could be. It ain't gonna ever be that with the Rangers around. I've had my own … my own problems with the gangs."

"You didn't have gang problems," Sly declared. "No way, no how!"

"I did, and I'll tell you kids 'nother time," Mr. Smith said. "Just know as much as you hate them gangbangers? I hate 'em more. Now, what Robin did with their money was dangerous, an' I can't encourage you kids to do more dangerous things."

Mr. Smith let the thought hang in the air as he gazed down at each of the kids in turn. To Robin, it felt like Mr. Smith wasn't just looking at him, but through him, right to the very core of his soul.

"But ... if you do decide to do the Robin Hood thing?" Mr. Smith repeated. "Well then, you got a partner in me. And it never hurts to have someone on your side who can pick any lock in the world. I'll see you kids later."

He limped out and closed the door behind him. For a moment, the kids looked at each other. Then Sly started dancing, waving his arms like the biggest hip-hop artist in Ironwood, Tone Def.

Robin in da house, Robin in da hood!
Robin in da house, Robin in da hood!

Doin' all the things dat he think
  he should!
Taking from the bad guys,
  givin' to the good,
He my main man, Robin in da hood!

Kaykay laughed. "Robin in da hood. I like that."

"Well, sure," Sly switched to his normal voice. " 'Cause he be a regular Robin Hood, and we be his Merry Gentlemen—and Merry Gentlewoman, I guess." He peered at Robin. "We really gonna steal from the rich, give to the poor? 'Cause if you want to, I'm in."

Robin was thoughtful. "If we do, we only steal from bad people. You can be rich and be a good person. Like you gonna be someday, Sly."

Sly smiled. "You got that right. So, what's our first job gonna be? And who's gonna get the money?"

Before he answered, Robin turned to Kaykay.

"You in?" he asked.

She nodded. Robin nodded back, then answered Sly. "I'm not sure," he said. "Maybe we lay low for a little bit. But I do know the community clinic is in trouble, and my grandma goes there for her doctor."

"Sounds good," Sly said. "Now, can we get out of this stinky room?"

Kaykay shook her head. "Go on. I gotta talk to Robin for a sec."

Sly took off. It was just Robin and Kaykay now.

"You did good, Robin," she said gently. "We all did good."

Then Kaykay did something shocking. She leaned in and kissed Robin softly on the cheek.

He felt hot blood rush to his head. He never, ever thought that she would ever—

Knock-knock-knock.

Three loud raps on the door broke the moment.

"Who's in there?!"

It was Sarge. Robin sheepishly opened the door.

"What are you doin' in there?" the head of the Center demanded.

"Talkin' 'bout a school assignment," Kaykay said quickly.

Assignment. That reminded Robin—he still had the *Bud, Not Buddy* vocab assignment to do for tomorrow. For himself and for Tyrone and Dodo.

"Well, talk later and join the fun," Sarge told them. "We're plannin' a big party for tomorrow. Christmas in September!"

Robin followed Kaykay out. Yes, there was a party to plan. But there was more to plan too. He needed to plan what to do with Tyrone and Dodo so he wouldn't be doing their homework for the rest of his life. He needed to plan how to take more money from the Rangers without them getting wise to him. He needed to plan who should get that scrilla once he and his crew got hold of it.

After all, he wasn't just Robin Paige anymore.

He was Robin in da hood.

Chapter Eleven

Tyrone? Dodo?"

It was free breakfast time on Wednesday morning, and Robin had just approached the football players' table, with Tyrone and Dodo's homework in hand.

He'd done it the night before, after telling his grandmother all about the "mystery donation" to the Center. She said the person who donated the money deserved a medal. Robin didn't say a word about how he was that person. The fewer people who knew, the better.

Tyrone and Dodo's *Not Buddy* vocab assignment was perfect. A-plus quality.

There's only one problem with it, Robin thought as he waited for a dumb football dude to finish the dirty joke he was telling. *It's exactly the same words, the same definitions, and the same sample sentences on both of them.*

"Commence," meaning "to start." From page five.

"Centipede," meaning "a long bug with a lot of legs." From page eighteen.

"Loathsome," meaning "worthy of disgust." From page one hundred thirty-six. For the sample sentence for "loathsome," Robin almost wrote, "Tyrone and Dodo are two loathsome dudes." Then he decided not to. It would be bad enough when Simesso saw their homework. They'd be so, so busted.

Well, I did what they asked me to do!

When the dirty joke ended, and the laughter wound down, Tyrone cleared his throat to get the guys' attention.

"Umm, Tyrone? Dodo? I got your, um, homework."

Tyrone glanced in his direction. "Yo! It's the shrimp! You comin' out for football? Know what? We could make you the kickoff tee!"

The other players cracked up. Robin seethed but tried to look afraid. He wanted to sucker these dudes so bad.

"You got our homework, Shrimp-tee?" Dodo asked.

"Uh-huh. I did one, just like you asked." Robin's voice quavered as he handed them each a folded sheet of notebook paper. Then he faced the other players, who were watching this scene with interest. "They asked me to do one for them."

"That's 'zactly right. One for us both!" Dodo shoved his homework inside his copy of *Bud, Not Buddy*. "That's 'cause Shrimp be our beeyotch."

"Shrimp be a good beeyotch. Get out of here, Shrimp," Tyrone ordered.

Mr. Simesso's class was first period again. Everyone put their homework on his desk and then sat to read a handout about Christopher Paul Curtis. Meanwhile, the teacher thumbed through their assignments. Robin read eagerly how the author of *Bud, Not Buddy* had worked on a car assembly line for years before he became a writer. There were pictures. Christopher Paul Curtis had dreadlocks in one of them.

I never knew an author could have dread—

Suddenly, Mr. Simesso's voice rang out.

"Tyrone Davis! Riondo Moore! Come up to my desk!"

The class ooh'd and tittered as Tyrone and Dodo made their way to the front. Before the two even got near his desk, Mr. Simesso went off on them.

"Gentlemen? If you're going to cheat? Cheat smart! Why would you turn in the exact same assignment, in the exact same handwriting? How stupid do you think I am? Or are you gentlemen just brain dead?"

The class laughed hard. Robin saw Kaykay and Sly grinning.

Dodo and Tyrone were so busted.

"You're getting zeros," Mr. Simesso told the two guys. "Do this again, you go to the principal. Now, sit down and try to have an original thought!"

Everyone tittered again as Tyrone and Dodo returned to their seats.

Tyrone growled at Robin as he passed by. "You think you so smart? We gonna git you, Shrimp!"

Sly suddenly spoke up. "It's get, Tyrone. Not 'git.' 'Get.' G-E-T. As in, 'Tyrone Davis, why don'chu get a life?' "

The class cracked up one more time.

Tyrone whirled at Sly. "I'm gonna git you too!"

Mr. Simesso banged his hand on his desk. "Tyrone and Riondo, in your seats! Everyone, do your work!"

The class quieted. Robin looked at Sly, so grateful that his ace had backed him up. Sly looked back at him and mouthed, "I hope you know what you doin'!"

Robin nodded. He knew what he was doing. Tyrone and Dodo were two scary dudes, for sure. But he was dreaming up a brilliant plan that could stop them in their tracks.

Let them try, he thought. *We'll be ready*.

"Dude, I want to thank you one more time," Robin told Sly. He, Sly, and Kaykay were walking north on Garvey toward the Center. "That was so def, standing up to Tyrone and Dodo like that."

"Hey, man. We're partners now," Sly assured him. Then he banged his knuckles twice against his own forehead. "Course, maybe I just had some temporary insanity."

Kaykay shook a finger at them. "It's not funny, dudes. Whatchu gonna do if Tyrone and Dodo come after you? You gonna let them jack you up?"

They were nearing the Center. Robin saw that a new banner had been stretched over the entrance:

THE CENTER IS SAVED!
MERRY XMAS IN SEPTEMBER!

"I got a plan. I'll tell you after the party," Robin promised his friends.

"Tell us now," Sly insisted.

Robin shook his head. "Nope. Let's have fun and not worry 'bout Tyrone and Dodo. I got them covered."

He thought he had them covered. He'd realized that if those dudes came after him and Sly, he'd remind them that he had Tyrone's science term paper rubric—the one with Tyrone's name on the front. If he went with it to the principal, or even Mr. Simesso, that could get Tyrone kicked off the football team easy. Maybe even kicked out of school. If Tyrone and Dodo really pushed it? He could always slip that rubric under the fake paver across the street from the Shrimp Shack, down in the same hole he'd found the Rangers' money. It had Tyrone's name in big letters on the front. The Rangers would think Tyrone had come back and left a calling card.

They'd mess him up. Bad.

No way would Tyrone risk that.

They pushed through the throng at the front door. Even though it was Wednesday afternoon, the Center was packed. While the kids had been in school, the place had been decorated with Christmas lights and ornaments. There was even a silver Christmas tree inside the front door. A buffet had been set up in the main entrance. Miz Paige had sent over some shrimp. Robin also saw ham, turkey, vegetables, pies, and a huge cake in the shape of Santa Claus. A boom box played Christmas music.

Robin and his friends went to the rec room. It was party central. Folks of all ages were dancing to the same old Motown that Miz Paige played in the Shrimp Shack. The kids stared at the old people busting moves like they were still teenagers. Sarge was the deejay. He saw the kids and gave a huge wave. Robin waved back.

Kaykay leaned in so Robin could hear over the loud music. "This is all 'cause of you, you know!"

" 'Cause of all of us!" Robin shouted back.

"Nope. 'Cause of you!" Kaykay insisted. The music shifted to something low and slow. "You wanna dance with me, Robin?"

He definitely wanted to dance with Kaykay. It would be a dream come true. But he saw Sly standing alone. Robin didn't want to leave his ace hanging.

"Dance with Sly," Robin suggested. "I'm gonna find Mr. Smith."

"You dancin' with me later, Robin," Kaykay scolded.

Robin grinned wildly. "I got a choice?"

"Nope!"

Kaykay took Sly's arm and led him onto the dance floor. Sly looked like he'd just died and gone to Christmas-in-September heaven.

Robin felt great. The Center was saved. He had a plan for Tyrone and Dodo. Kaykay liked him. She liked him a lot.

Suddenly—out of nowhere!—his grandmother's words from the day before yesterday roared back at him.

"You play with fire, you get yo'self burned!"

Robin gulped, the good feelings shooting out of him like air from a popped balloon. He was playing with fire all over the place. He was sassing Tyrone and Dodo. He was thinking about stealing more gang money. If they didn't want to get burned, he and his crew had to be careful.

Super careful.

Okay. He steadied himself. *We can do that*.

"Hey there, Robin in the hood."

Mr. Smith had come up behind him. He was wearing a tie for the party, though he'd loosened it so it hung down low. "How be the secret superhero? This jus' the beginning!"

Robin allowed himself to smile. Mr. Smith was right. It was just the beginning. He and his friends would have to be crazy careful, but there was so much good that they could—

"Robin Paige!"

Robin turned around. Two beefy guys— one white, one black—stood with folded arms. They wore identical black pants, white shirts, and blue windbreakers, with IRONWOOD PD in huge yellow letters on the back.

"Can we help you?" Mr. Smith asked the men.

Both guys flashed silver badges that made Robin's knees weak.

"Officer Goodall, Ironwood police," the black guy said.

"Office Leedham, Ironwood PD," the white guy barked. "Robin Paige, you're coming with us!"

The two cops grabbed Robin's arms.

"What'd I do?" Robin shouted, panicked. "What'd I do?"

The cops didn't answer; they just dragged him toward a side door. As they did, Robin saw his friends quit dancing and stare with shock at what was happening.

What do they want with me? Where are they taking me?

"Am I under arrest?" Robin gasped.

The cops said nothing, just tightened their grips on his arm.

"Answer me!" Robin screamed, twisting this way and that.

"You let that boy go!" Mr. Smith demanded.

"Get out of my face, you old geezer!" The white guy shoved Mr. Smith away.

Oh my God! Robin had a scary thought. *What if these aren't real cops? What if the Rangers figured out I'd taken the money and sent fake cops to grab me and take me to them? I'm gonna die!*

"Help!" Robin yelled to his friends and Mr. Smith, who were trailing behind him and the huge cops. "Don't let these dudes take me away!" Robin screamed as the two beefy guys dragged him through the side door. "Help! Help mee-eeee!"